Kaya's Journey

First published in India in 2019 by HarperCollins Children's Books
An imprint of HarperCollins *Publishers*
A-75, Sector 57, Noida, Uttar Pradesh 201301, India
www.harpercollins.co.in

2 4 6 8 10 9 7 5 3 1

Text © Mila Kahlon 2019
Illustrations © HarperCollins *Publishers* India 2019

P-ISBN: 978-935-357-322-5

Typeset in 11.5/14.5 Palatino
by Isha Nagar

Printed and bound at Replika Press Pvt. Ltd.

Kaya's Journey

The Story of a 100-year-old Koi Fish

Mila Kahlon

Illustrated by Paridhi Didwania

HarperCollins*Children'sBooks*

To my beautiful niece,
Kaya

And inspired by my children,
Ravibir and Bella

In a land far, far away called Canada, Avani woke up from the strong rays of the sun on her face. She could hear droplets of melting snow falling from the rooftop onto the ground and the pitter patter of icicles turning into water in the trees and bushes outside her window. She peeked at her twin brother, Niam, fast asleep in his bed and realised it was the weekend! No school and no alarms!

Just as she started to slip back under the covers to sleep some more, there was a tap on the door.

'Hey guys, it's grandpa! I am awake before you and I think I will win the bet this year! You will have to roast marshmallows for me!'

The bet? The bet!

Avani jumped out of bed and shook her brother awake. 'Wake up! The ice has melted! We have to go look for Kaya!'

Avani and Niam darted towards the door and pushed it open, almost toppling grandpa Yogi over. Still in their night suits, they ran downstairs, put on their gumboots and rushed outside.

The entire farm was glistening with dewdrops and patches of melting snow and ice. Tufts of green grass peeked through the thawing earth.

Spring was finally here! And with spring came the time for the family's favourite tradition.

The children soon reached the shore of a small lake in the middle of the property and stood there catching their breath as they carefully studied the surface. They saw tadpoles, some small fish, frogs and a few birds. But not what they were looking for. 'Patience,' said grandpa, who had caught up with them and was resting on a big rock close by. 'Keep looking.'

Suddenly there was a golden shimmer in a distant part of the lake. The kids strained their eyes to see what it was. They wondered if the rays of the sun were playing tricks on them. But the shimmering shape moved again. Then they both shouted together, 'I saw her first!'

'No, it was me!'

'Calm down, calm down!' said grandpa softly. 'This year she made sure you both saw her at the same time. She is very smart.'

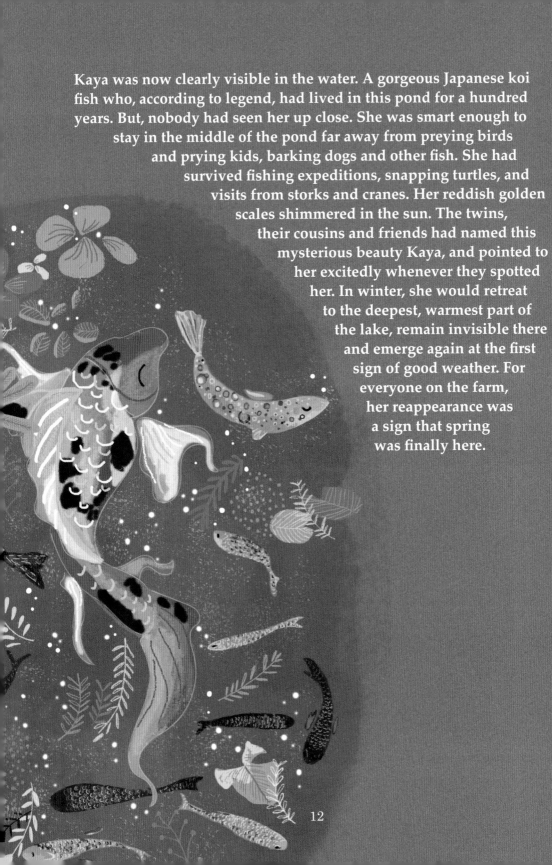

Kaya was now clearly visible in the water. A gorgeous Japanese koi fish who, according to legend, had lived in this pond for a hundred years. But, nobody had seen her up close. She was smart enough to stay in the middle of the pond far away from preying birds and prying kids, barking dogs and other fish. She had survived fishing expeditions, snapping turtles, and visits from storks and cranes. Her reddish golden scales shimmered in the sun. The twins, their cousins and friends had named this mysterious beauty Kaya, and pointed to her excitedly whenever they spotted her. In winter, she would retreat to the deepest, warmest part of the lake, remain invisible there and emerge again at the first sign of good weather. For everyone on the farm, her reappearance was a sign that spring was finally here.

'Grandpa, grandpa! Please tell us the story again, please!' begged Avani and Niam.

Grandpa Yogi settled down on the rock, pulled on his woollen scarf and let out a sigh. 'It's a long and beautiful story. Let's hope we are not late for breakfast. Your mom will not be happy.'

'No, grandpa, please tell us, we will not interrupt!'

'Fine, kids. Listen up ...'

'Kaya was one of her kind in her pond in Canada. A hundred years earlier, a Japanese gardener had brought her to the new land where he finally wanted to settle. Kaya was a very special creature. This tiny and seemingly fragile fish had braved many dangers and hardships to follow her dream of seeing the world. Her story became the stuff of legend, revered in many cultures as a symbol of courage and perseverance.

The man who hired the gardener had been fortunate to get a plot of land surrounded by a lush forest, within which nestled a big clear sparkling lake. It was within this lake that Kaya made her home and from where she silently observed what was going on above the water. The land flourished. And many generations lived there in love, happiness and prosperity. And with each generation the legend of the big golden fish lived on.

Kaya and her brothers and sisters hatched in a peaceful pond in China. The Chinese called her kind of pretty fish 'carp'. Kaya's father was a huge black-coloured carp. Their mother sparkled in gorgeous red and orange hues. Her brothers were all a gentle white and blue. And Kaya and her sisters twirled around showing off their red and pink spots.

Everyone was happy growing up in the pond, eating off the bountiful bottom, playing, jumping and swimming under the huge waterlily plants. Nobody disturbed them there. And everybody was content.

Kaya was unlike her parents and siblings. While everyone was busy with their routine, she tried to sneak out to the surface of the pond and steal a glimpse of the shore. The trees seemed tall and different with strange birds landing on them. Small, unfamiliar animals came forward to drink water at the pond. Sometimes while swimming, Kaya came under the shadow of a huge tree growing nearby.

As she looked up at its branches and leaves, the sun sparkled through and she spotted the blue of the sky. She wondered about the big unknown world out there. There was a longing in her little heart that never ceased. A longing to discover the world beyond the pond.

Her siblings made fun of her as they could not believe there
could be anything more exciting beyond their small universe.
Her parents worried about her wanderlust and
tried to warn her about the dangers that
lurked around. Kaya was scared,
but her desire to explore was
stronger than her fear.

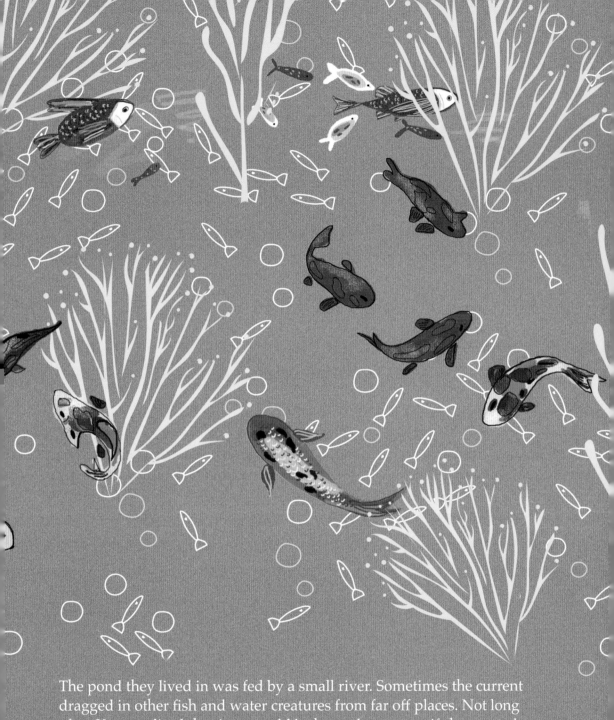

The pond they lived in was fed by a small river. Sometimes the current dragged in other fish and water creatures from far off places. Not long after, Kaya realised the river would be her only way out if she wanted to explore the rest of the world. But every time she tried to swim up against the current, the water pushed her back into the pond.

Kaya didn't give up. She made sure she ate well and got enough exercise during the day to get stronger and bigger. Every night, she imagined herself swimming up the river and discovering amazing new worlds. She kept trying. Inspired, some of her brothers and sisters joined in. Until one day, with a big push, they found themselves swimming upstream.

The journey was tough. The riverbed was very different from the pond. Sometimes it was clear and friendly, at other times the waters became murky and angry. Long slippery plants tried to entangle the fish, and huge rocks and mysterious predators tried to catch them. But the unknown was as exciting as it was scary.

One day the fish came to a spot where the current became so strong, it almost seemed violent. The water was ice cold and the little fish popped their heads out to see where they had reached. What they saw was a waterfall – a huge, terrifying and deafeningly noisy mass of water. And sparkling on top of it was a giant, golden manmade gate. Was that the end of their journey?

Kaya and her siblings gathered in a circle to decide what to do. It seemed useless to keep swimming under the waterfall when there was no other way further upstream. A few of them felt they had had enough adventure and wanted to go back to the pond. Then Kaya had an idea. Swimming up the current had made them stronger, faster and smarter. Why give up now? Why not try and jump over the waterfall and complete the journey? Most of Kaya's siblings laughed at the idea and decided to return home. But, a few braver ones stayed back to give it a try.

The little fish kept jumping up the waterfall, trying to reach the top. For months, then years, they kept jumping and leaping. But they could not propel themselves high enough. Exhausted, one by one, they gave up and went back home to rest. Until only Kaya was left. For the first time in her life she was alone. She felt scared and missed her family. But she also wanted to make them proud.

Kaya continued to jump. There were days when she was so tired that she was ready to let herself be dragged by the current back to her home. But there was a fire inside her which didn't let her give up. What she did not realise was that with every jump, her muscles were becoming stronger, her body more flexible and agile, her mind sharper, her lungs more powerful and she could endure more effort without getting tired. Until one day, a huge, final, incredible leap lifted her right over the waterfall and the gate which stood above it.

What Kaya didn't know was that all the while she was trying to leap over the waterfall, the gods had been watching her in amazement. Many times, they placed bets between themselves that Kaya would give up the next day. But every time they came back to check on her, they found her still working hard and trying to find her way up. They could not believe their eyes and admired the courage and perseverance of this little creature.

They had seen incredible strength in lions, tigers, rhinos and eagles. But never in an ordinary fish. Regardless of her size, shape and species, Kaya was determined to fulfil her dream. So instead of betting against her, the gods soon started betting that she would succeed the next day … and the next … and the next.

The day she finally did, a huge celebration erupted in the skies and the gods descended to meet this incredible fish and reward her for her inspiring strength.

One of them turned her colour from pink to bright, sparkling gold, so that she would stand out amongst all other fish.

Another adorned her body with a tattoo of a dragon – a symbol of invincibility. They then named the gate on top of the waterfall Dragon Gate in her honour.

The third gave her beautiful, big fins which floated around her like lace. And finally, the gods changed the name of her species from 'carp' to the more dignified and respectful 'koi' fish.

Now in the country of Japan, Kaya continued her journey through more peaceful waters until she wandered into a rice paddy field where a farmer, knee deep in water, was tending to his crops. Curious, Kaya swam close to him to examine this strange two-legged creature.

The farmer was poor and had children to feed. When he saw this huge, robust, gold-coloured fish, he was overjoyed as she meant a generous dinner for his family. He caught Kaya and ran home to his wife, asking her to immediately put a pot of water to boil over the fire. He put Kaya on a big wooden chopping board and prepared the knife to gut her.

But his hand stopped mid-air as the farmer could not believe what he was seeing. Kaya was lying there without flapping and gasping for breath. Instead, she was calmly looking straight into his eyes, ready to accept her destiny. Her unflinching expression reminded the farmer of the samurai warriors who were revered in his culture and famous for not blinking an eye even in the face of certain death.

The farmer could not bring himself to kill Kaya. Instead, he gently lifted her from the chopping board and released her back into the water of his rice field. From that day onwards, Kaya and the farmer coexisted peacefully and happily. Kaya ate the pests and creatures that gnawed at the rice plants, and the farmer was happy to be able to watch this incredible beauty day after day.

After sparing the fish, the farmer had more kindness and generosity in his heart. He smiled more and worked harder, and his land prospered. He was no longer poor. This truly special creature had brought good luck to him and his family.

His children started drawing pictures of Kaya and flying koi-shaped kites with paper fins that floated gracefully in the air.

With time, the story of the amazing koi spread through the village and people from far and near came to see the legendary 'samurai' fish. One look at Kaya made them realise she was somehow magical. Since they could not have a Kaya of their own, they tattooed her image on their shoulders, chests and backs. In this way, they would be able to look at her every single day and be as courageous and strong as her.

The story reached the ears of the leader of the samurai himself. He took a seven-day journey on horseback to descend to the paddy field from the top of the mountain to meet Kaya. Upon examining her closely, the samurai noticed the dragon tattoo on her body and immediately knew this fish had a higher purpose.

The farmer knew Kaya had done her work in his field, his heart and his family. He bowed down to her and with tears in his eyes he allowed the samurai to fill a huge bucket of water and take Kaya on the next leg of her incredible journey.

On the way, the group of samurai was attacked by the Emperor's guard and managed to run away. But the cart, carrying Kaya along with provisions for the severe mountain winter, was captured by the soldiers. The soldiers were equally mesmerized by the gorgeous fish and took her straight to the Emperor in Tokyo. The Emperor not only had a keen eye for beauty, he also believed in omens and good luck charms. Therefore, he ordered Kaya to be released into the moat running around his palace for extra protection and blessings. A gardener was appointed to look after her.

The gardener grew more and more attached to Kaya. Sometimes he touched her body and felt the scars she had acquired from her long journey to Japan. In her eyes, he saw the wisdom of long years and the experience of many roads travelled and things seen beyond his imagination. He had never left Tokyo and Kaya's wanderlust was contagious. He looked at the dragon tattooed on her body and promised himself to be brave and leave Tokyo one day and explore the big wide world.

One day, a wealthy Canadian politician came to Tokyo to see the cherry blossoms. Canada was a country with abundant land for farming and life in the outdoors. The politician came to stay with the Emperor and learn and observe the fine art of Japanese gardening. He was so keen to transfer this knowledge to Canada that he offered to employ the humble gardener on his farm near Toronto. The gardener bowed in front of the Emperor and asked him to let him go. He had a few more years left of being able to work hard and travel and see a world beyond Japan. Moved by the gardener's plight, the Emperor gave his blessings. The Emperor knew that the gardener was very attached to Kaya and allowed him to take the fish along, to always remind him of his homeland. Overawed by the Emperor's generosity, the gardener fell at his feet and wept, for he truly couldn't imagine being separated from Kaya.

It didn't take long for the gardener to realise that his new home on the farm in Canada was a blessed, happy place. The farm had a huge lake which became Kaya's home. It also had a brick house filled with children, love and laughter, and a piece of land for him to turn into a Zen garden. He spent the last years of his life tending to the garden and checking on Kaya every single day. Funnily enough, he felt that she was looking after him rather than he looking after her. She seemed to have settled in just fine in the lake, amongst the new species of fish, plants and birds. Kaya led a quiet, solitary life. But she was never lonely. From under the water she could observe the lives of the people on the farm and how things changed with each passing generation. Just like us right now … Make no mistake … She is watching us.'

Grandpa Yogi cleared his throat and stretched his legs. The twins were listening intently. 'Just like Kaya, the two of you can always find the courage and strength to jump over your own Dragon Gate. Whenever you feel that you are faced with a difficult obstacle, think of her, think of yourselves as a koi fish – and don't give up, keep trying, and get out of the shallow waters and transform yourselves into a dragon. Don't get discouraged by others, follow your dreams and they will come true. Kaya is here to remind us of that every single day.'

Just at that moment, Avani and Niam's mom called out for breakfast. Slowly, keeping pace with their grandfather, they started walking home, already planning how to squeeze as many adventures as possible into the next twelve hours. Kaya watched on as the three shapes faded into the distance and contentedly flapped her fins, enjoying the rays of sunshine upon her back. It was a new day.

Why Koi Fish Are Really Special ...

The story of the koi fish shows that you can overcome life's obstacles and adversities if you have patience and tenacity.

China is the true birth place of this fish. When the fish was first presented to the Japanese, they saw the koi's great potential and started breeding them for their brilliant colours. The koi fish were considered the perfect gift for the Emperor's imperial palace moat in 1914.

Extremely resilient, koi fish have the ability to survive and adapt to various climates and water conditions. These fish have been accidentally or purposely released in the wild in every continent except Antarctica and have thus spread through the world.

The koi got their name in 500 bc but the fish itself 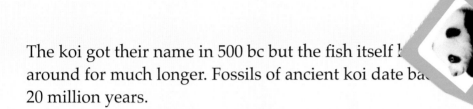 around for much longer. Fossils of ancient koi date ba..
20 million years.

'Koi' means affection and love. Therefore, these fish are a symbol of friendship in Japan. But because of the lone koi that made it to the top of the waterfall, they symbolise strength, character, individuality, courage to attain even seemingly impossible goals and fulfilled destiny.

Koi fish are a common symbol in Chinese culture and feng shui, and are depicted in artwork, clothing and tattoos.

At the annual Boy Festival in Japan, colourful streaming koi shaped kites and flags represent members of the family. Black – father; red and orange – mother; blue and white – son; red and pink – daughter.

MILA KAHLON

Bulgaria-born Mila Kahlon dreamt of being a published writer since the age of 8. Writing of secret diaries, poems and daydreaming of fictional characters later found an outlet in journalism. She spent more than 15 years working in print media as a correspondent and assistant editor in Bulgaria, France and India, before permanently settling down in the city of Mumbai with her husband, two kids, dog and guinea pig. A stroke of inspiration fuelled the writing of this story and finally Mila's lifelong desire took life. This book was inspired by her children and aims to show them that a dream is achievable no matter how small or big you are.

PARIDHI DIDWANIA

Having a passion for textile prints, Paridhi Didwania believes that design fosters a culture of creativity. A die-hard colour enthusiast, she makes use of striking palettes to bring her design to life. She has worked extensively with artisans, developing block prints for various companies. Paridhi also loves illustrating for children's books and is greatly inspired by nature.